Lost Memories

Hugo Sharman

CONTENTS

Chapter 1

Elainne Winfield is who I am. I'm the only child of Jasmine and Theodore Winfield, and I'm eighteen years old. I'm a senior in high school and should graduate in a few months. However, I don't want to attend college when I graduate because I'd rather stay local and start looking for a job right away. In addition, I like to read and create art, particularly paper crafts and pottery.

Or, at the very least, that's what they said.

The question "Honey, are you ready?" I'm startled out of my thoughts by a voice. Turning to face the woman in the doorway, I find myself gradually sinking lower into the firm mattress I'm sitting on.

She is merely a stranger to me, despite the fact that she has been by my side for the past two weeks. I don't perceive many similarities between us despite the fact that we are related by blood. Most of the doctors continued telling me I look a lot like my mother, despite the fact that her chestnut hair is shorter and darker than mine, her eyes are a different colour, and our faces are not the same shape.

After a minute of stillness, I mutter, "I am. I get out of bed when she calls out to me.

She whispers, "Let's go. Your dad went outside to collect the automobile after we were through with the paperwork. I can practically hear a whisper in her voice, and I can feel it encompassing me as I approach her.

We exit the room and enter the hospital's dismal hallway. She tenderly places her arm across my shoulders, and I let her lead the way without thinking. Uncomfortable static fills my head, drowning out all of my thoughts, and I am oblivious to everything going on around me. When my mother enters the door, I don't glance up from my feet and instead feel a change in the atmosphere.

Instead of the oppressive hospital odour, we are greeted by the pleasant aroma of April. Despite it being the beginning of spring, it feels like summer because of the temperature.

I spy a man lying against his car not far from the hospital entrance, his crossed arms resting on his chest. He dashes over to our side as soon as he notices my mother and I leaving.

He asks me, "Do you need a hand?"

"No, no problem. I'm able to walk by myself. He takes my other side and supports me as I go to the car even if I shake my head. As soon as I get in, he and my mother go into the front seats, and before I know it, we're leaving the hospital.

The journey is silent. We all seem to be aware of the awkwardness between us yet don't seem to want to strike up a discussion.

I've known the two people in front of me all my life, but they are only strangers. a life that I am now ignorant of. I try to remember something from my history once more in an effort to discover something I can hold onto, but I'm unsuccessful. It is all vacant.

You still have some recollections. Your mind is not completely erased. Consider it as sorting your memories into various boxes. When something significant occurred, your brain locked them up and moved them out of your grasp so that you could cope with it. Before that, they were all neatly stored away. Each box needs a key to be unlocked, but there are many of them. Some of them may appear to you by chance while you are in a familiar setting or are exposed to something you are accustomed to. You merely need some time and mental rest for some of them. However, some keys might be lost forever.

While I was still in the hospital, my psychiatrist said some things to me that come to mind. She claims that I suffer from a specific sort of amnesia, the term of which escapes me at the moment. I'm not completely sure what my brain is meant to be recovering from, but she mentioned it might take some time for it to process what occurred to me.

I only learned that I and another buddy of mine had been abducted when I awoke in the hospital, very disoriented. After being absent for five weeks, I suddenly reappeared. The youngster was still missing when someone took me to the hospital after discovering me close to the road leading outside of the town. How did those five weeks unfold?

When the quiet buzz of the car engine stops, I immediately become aware of my surroundings. We are parked in front of a sizable house with a light pink front, as I can see from the window. Do we own it? Nothing at all comes to mind when I see it.

I follow my folks as they get out of the car. Despite my assurances that I can walk just fine on my own, they immediately rush to my side to assist me. It's not like I was hurt, really. I just had a few scrapes and bruises when I was taken to the hospital, but they have since completely recovered.

Once more, they take both of my sides, as though to protect me from everything around us. My mother struggles in her pocket till she eventually pulls out a key as we approach the door. She opens the door, and we walk right through into a small corridor.

I try to find something in the corridor that will trigger a memory somewhere in my brain, but all of my searches are in vain. Nothing feels comfortable enough, not even the coat hanger in the corner or the shoe rack.

My dad asks me, "Are you going to take off your shoes?" They have already swapped out their uncomfortable shoes for some cosy slippers, as I can see when I look down.

I say, "Oh, right," as I stoop to collect my laces.

My mother's worried voice reaches me, "Do you need any help with them?"

In response, I shake my head, but a mild sensation of dizziness prevents me. "No, it's okay; I have it." While my mother hands me my slippers, I unlace my shoes and set them aside. Nothing about them feels like mine since they are soft but frigid.

My parents lead me to the living room from the hallway. I make an effort to take it all in and look for anything familiar, but all I can make out is how cosy the space seems. On one side of the room, there is a huge beige couch, and on the other, there is one of those electric fires. A giant TV is mounted on the wall above it, and its top is adorned with a variety of small decorations. One single armchair and a little glass table are situated close to the couch on the plush carpet.

My mother finally asks, "So?" and I turn to face them. They appear to be waiting for me to announce that a miracle has occurred and that I now remember everything from the way they stare at me, which I can see. I don't, though.

I just shook my head. Despite the room's beige and white colour scheme making it appear cosy and homely, my brain hasn't yet registered it as a place to call home. It doesn't feel at all familiar; rather, I feel as though I'm seeing it for the first time.

"All right, let me take you to your room. Maybe you'll recognise that one," she says again as she joins our arms. I consented to her escorting me up the stairs and out of the living room. We pass by several pictures hanging on the wall next to us as we ascend, but we move too rapidly for me to see what's on them.

I notice four identical doors as we move down the corridor. Would I correctly identify which one was mine if I had to pause and guess?

To my luck, we halt in front of the second one after passing the first one on our left. My mum invites me inside by opening the door. I pause for a few moment before following her inside.

The room isn't very noteworthy. The typical furnishings are present, including a bed, a good desk with a matching chair and a stack of textbooks on top of it, another plush carpet, a sizable closet and a mirror. In addition, a modest bookcase in the room's corner holds three rows of orderly-arranged books. The simplicity of the space is broken by their vibrant spines, which catch my attention.

I slowly turn to look around and discover that there are less items there than I had anticipated. It is spotless, as one might anticipate from a girl's room, but it lacks character. Only one framed photo is on the nightstand, and there are no other decorations or personal touches in the room.

I turn to face my mother when I feel her watchful eyes on me. Her small smile only seems to highlight the message of hope that is etched all over her face.

I reply, "Nothing," to her. I find it difficult to really put my finger on anything because it feels kind of empty.

She makes an effort to hide her disappointment, but I can tell. Oh, don't worry, you'll recall it in due time. You've always preferred it this way despite my repeated requests for you to add more colour and beautify the space. She gives me a brief wistful smile before gathering her composure and leading me back downstairs.

As I wait for her to finish eating dinner in the living room, I make an effort to ignore the nagging feeling of guilt in my chest. Until he finally settles down on the other side of the couch and begins watching TV, my dad wanders around the house. As we sit there, he keeps giving me brief glances, but I pretend I'm not noticing them as I aimlessly scan the space.

We eat meals in quiet with only the occasional forced remark or two, so it isn't much different. It's difficult for me to talk to them about anything, and they aren't any less reluctant than I am, despite how much I want to. I can't say I'm at fault for them. After all, their only child has barely even retained their identity after going absent for more than a month.

My mother eventually speaks, darting a glimpse at me before asking, "How's the food?"

I finish my bite and then respond. "I like it. Absolutely superior to hospital food.

Only a few—somehow much more awkward—hums are elicited in response to my terrible humour attempt. As soon as I complete my meal and retire to my room, I almost sigh with relief.

I find some solace in the comfortable mattress as I look up at the ceiling. Although my parents are doing their best to make me feel secure at home, even when I was still in the hospital, I was already accustomed to this environment. I slowly become overwhelmed by the hazy memories of the hospital and the various exams, but one of them resurfaces and swiftly eclipses the others.

I get out of bed and cross the room to the mirror on the other side. I struggle with my attire as I stand there and eventually open my top to see my protruding ribs. I eventually manage to make out the phrases etched on my skin.

When I was in the hospital, I first saw it. I had no idea that some black ink was permanently adorning my flesh before then. a body ink.

The first people to notice it were the doctors. They questioned me about it to see if I understood what it meant, but like everything else, I didn't. I was expecting them to notify my parents or the police about it, but no one did, so I made the decision to keep it a secret for the time being. "r. p.if you forget" is delicately touched by my finger since I feel they hold a deeper significance for me.

CHAPTER 2

"Elainne!"

As I enter the dark room, the voice is audible all around me. Providing I can get away.

"Elainne!"

In front of me, a petite woman appears. She tightens her grip on my arms, and I'm too shocked to react. I can only stare at her tear-streaked face.

"What have you done to my son?" the mother asked. She shakes me so violently that my vision becomes hazy.

I haven't done anything, you know. My voice sounds hoarse and empty when I respond, like if it isn't even mine.

She yells back at me, "Liar!" "Give me back my son!" you cry.

A man suddenly emerges by her side as I blink. My heart clenches as I see their helpless expressions. I take a slow step back, but they quickly close the gap in front of us. Their features melt and morph into hideous creatures that stare back at me. Their scalded hands extend towards me.

I scream, "P-please... I don't know where he is."

A distorted voice asks, "Who are you, Elainne?" I, who? That is a valid query.

"I don't know," you say. When my back strikes the wall, I stoop and cover my face with my hands until I can no longer see them. Why won't they simply disappear? Please let me leave.

Once more, the forms merge and shift, and instead of the short woman, I find myself in front of someone far more recognisable. the mother. My father is standing next to her, and their shadows viciously loom over me.

Up until I spot a boy's form in the distance, my heart beats even faster and I feel like I'm shrinking even more.

Although his face is covered in tears, he is lighted and bathed in a warm glow like a beacon. He yells, "Elainne," after me. He speaks softly, yet I can still make him out as though he were right next to me.

My mother yells at me in the faint accented voice of the woman, "Give me back my child!" I scream as a clawed hand lunges out to grab me.

I jolt awake in my bed, gasping for air. Just a nightmare, that's all.

I gradually get used to the darkness and can now see the surroundings. In my bedroom I am. There isn't a pitch-black space ready to engulf me. It's okay.

But despite that, I keep thinking about the boy's face as I return to the family from my dream. Christy Young. the companion I was abducted with.

And the only individual whose face I briefly recognised.

I was a key piece of evidence in the inquiry because I was the only one to escape from our captors, but I didn't even know my identity, let alone what had happened to us. His parents insisted on coming to see me nonetheless, and I immediately understood why when I saw them come into my room. I'm not sure how, but there was one thing that was plainly written all across their faces—despair.

"Elainne," the woman had remarked as she and her husband cautiously walked up to my hospital bed. Jia Zhou introduced herself as she pointed to the man to her right and said, "This is my husband, Logan. We... we heard what happened to you. Although you might not recall us, we have already crossed paths. We are Chris' parents, Christian.

Unlike their warped incarnations in my nightmare, both of them were friendly to me, but it didn't do much to fix my shattered memory.

Prior to her showing me the picture.

The young man, Chris, was standing with his hands in his pockets and a big grin on his face. The image was very different from the one the cops had. That picture, which just displayed his face and concealed any feelings behind a neutral look, was probably taken from the school yearbook.

However, this image gave us a different look at him. The fact that I instantly recognised this youngster when I saw his photo wasn't so much a memory as it was a gut instinct.

Do you have any information? Please?" His mother was pleading with me for whatever information I could offer, which wasn't much. The boy's father approached her side and placed a kind hand on her shoulder. As I waited for my response, I saw the pair try to hold back their tears.

I turned my head away and could only muster a head shake. I apologised to them. I made the decision to ignore my gut feeling because intuition couldn't be of any use to anyone. The only thing they wanted was to have their kid returned, and nothing I felt could do that.

Even though it was upsetting, the brief interaction had a greater impact than the police's repeated questioning. I once again experience the same feeling of dread in my stomach at the mere notion of that.

I was immediately bombarded with inquiries after regaining consciousness in the hospital, including: do I recall what happened the night I was abducted; do I recognise the boy in the image; and do I recall anyone—known or unknown—approaching us or following us. One of the officers was extremely pushy, but when they realised I didn't understand what they were saying, they were all disappointed. Their most crucial piece of information proved to be useless.

I remember that there were other people who came to see me besides Chris's parents. My pals from my class visited a couple occasions. At the time, the number of unfamiliar faces was overwhelming, yet I was nevertheless appreciative of their assistance.

A girl named Jane was the first to arrive. I have a hard time recalling her last name. Kingston, perhaps? It appears to be Kingston. She was one of several who came and wished me well and was also the one who came the most often.

The memories she told me about my time in high school before the kidnapping were more priceless than the flowers or the numerous "Get well soon" cards that I received during those trips. She turned out to be one of my best friends, which accounted for her regular visits.

She once said to me as she put fresh flowers in the vase by my bed, "I mean, I can't say you were exactly popular—you're definitely popular now, though—but the people liked you." Why else would they keep visiting you and sending you presents on a regular basis?

My parents and carers informed me about all the people who wanted to visit me, but they were rare for me, especially in the first few days, so her words made perfect sense to me. Despite this, Jane occasionally brought a few students with her, but in my recall, their faces were simply a blur and nothing that I could pick out; it's still the same.

Why was Chris the only one I even somewhat remembered? Was it the remorse I felt for not having any information that might have helped the police or his parents?

The enigma surrounding Chris and his departure taints the ideal picture I've thus far imagined, sending my head into a tailspin since, despite my best efforts, I can't seem to solve it. Later, when I try to go back to sleep, I continue to think about it as the previous nightmare lingers in the back of my mind.

Chapter 3

"Honey, you have a visitor." My mom's voice echoes through my room from the other side of the door.

"Who is it?" I ask in confusion. This is the first time anyone's visiting me since I returned home, so I wonder who it might be.

She opens the door and peeks inside. "It's your friend from the hospital, Jane."

"Oh," I only mutter in surprise, even though she should be the most probable choice. "I'll be there in a minute."

When I descend the stairs and step into the living room, I spot Jane sitting on the couch and chatting with Mom. As soon as she notices me, though, she greets me with a wide smile.

"Oh, Elainne! Hi! I haven't seen you in so long," she says as she stands up from the couch, even though we've last seen each a week ago. However, I decide not to comment on that, and instead return her enthusiastic greeting.

Mom quickly leaves us and slips into the kitchen, while we sit on the couch and start chatting. Soon after, she returns with a plate full of cookies that she places on the table in front of us.

"I made these with my mom, so I brought some to you," Jane tells me as she reaches for the plate and grabs a cookie. "You should try them. It's not because I made them, but they're really, really good." To prove her statement, she takes a bite of it, the enjoyment visible on her face.

Convinced, I follow her example and let out a happy hum as the chocolate chips melt in my mouth. We sit in silence for a minute, each nibbling on her own cookie, until she finally finishes hers and starts speaking again.

"I'm sorry I can't stay too long, I just wanted to stop by and see how you're doing. Oh, and I have something for you too." She reaches for the armchair, and for the first time, I notice a handbag resting on it. "Some people heard I planned to stop by, so they asked me to give you some stuff," she mumbles as she rummages through her bag.

Soon enough, she has a tiny stack of cards in her hand, and I inwardly beam at the thought of all the people who made an effort to write as much as a couple of words and pass them on to Jane.

"Okay, let's see," she begins, looking at the first card in her hand. "This one's from Natalie Ross, this one's from Penelope Atkins, then there's this one from Evan Brooks..." Jane lists out the names that mean nothing to me, and I sigh a little breath of relief when she gets to the very last name from the pile.

I accept the stack from her, and then put it on the table right next to her cookies. Just when I'm about to thank her, she cuts in.

"I should probably get going now, but it was nice to see you again. Do you have a new phone?" Jane asks as she gets up from the couch.

I nod reluctantly. "I do, but I don't use it that often."

"Oh, great! We can exchange numbers then. That way, I can give you a heads up the next time I visit. Maybe I'll bring someone else with me, everyone misses you so much."

She produces two slips of paper from her bag, along with a pen that she offers to me. I write down my number, triple checking for a mistake. When I don't seem to find any, I gave the pen back to her, and then we exchange the slips.

With the last few pleasantries, I follow her to the door and give her a quick wave goodbye when she leaves. Now alone, I leave my mom in the kitchen and go back to my room, heading straight for my desk.

I slump into the chair just like I did earlier today, and pick up an abandoned notebook from the desk's shiny surface. When Jane arrived, I've just started flipping through its pages and glancing over its contents. It was one of my school notebooks, packed with notes from my classes, all written in a neat, slightly cursive handwriting.

There isn't anything meaningful inside, but I don't even expect to get much from them, except an inevitable headache. It isn't that much about giving myself a refresher on our school's curriculum as much as it is about testing my own limits and seeing how long I can go on without feeling that dull pain inside my head.

As if summoned, it appears again, albeit not as intense at first. With a frustrated sigh, I close the notebook and put it back in its original place.

This happened all the time. I was very quick to get headaches, and my head would start to spin if I read or started at a screen for too long, just like now.

I glance at the forgotten smartphone sitting on the far left end of the desk, right next to my old laptop. Both of them are useless to me in their own ways. The laptop is still in function, but I need a password to unlock it, one which I obviously don't remember. And since my old phone wasn't by my side when I was found—it was most likely destroyed long ago—my parents got me a new one. At first they were reluctant about it, but I promised not to use it often. After all, social media doesn't pose much of a distraction to me because I don't have any.

So, now that I have a lot of free time, I still find myself staring at the ceiling, trying to chase away my boredom.

I look over to my small bookshelf, letting my eyes graze over the spines. I read the titles, but they mean nothing to me. Have I read all of these books before? Or were they just sitting still and collecting dust on the small shelves?

Knowing that they're also useless at the moment, I turn to the only source of entertainment I have left: the tattoo.

It's been almost a week since I came back from the hospital, and its mystery is still lingering in my mind. I stand up from the desk and stretch my muscles, then walk over to the mirror again, just like I did many times in these past few days.

With the faint light of an April afternoon coming through my window, I can't see it that clearly, but it's already etched into my mind. My fingers trace it, and I find myself curious. Even though it's my tattoo, I wonder what's the story behind it. But most importantly, what does "r. p." mean.

Is it a person? Someone who magically knows my entire life story and could help me remember everything I forgot? Or is it a thing, an object that somehow contains all of my memories? I wonder if something like that even exists. If it does, why is no one talking about it?

I search through my limited memories, trying to pinpoint anything that fits those letters. If they're supposed to be someone's initials, then I have no luck whatsoever. I can't remember talking to or hearing about anyone whose initials fit, so I shift my focus on objects. Even then, the possibilities seem both scarce and endless at the same time.

Finally giving up of the tattoo as well, I decide to go downstairs and grab some water. Leaving my discarded slippers aside, I tiptoe out of my room. I pass my parents' bedroom and head down the stairs when a voice stops me.

"We can't keep doing this, Theodore!" It's my mother's voice, but it's not as gentle as it is when she talks to me. It's hushed, but also much angrier than I've ever heard it.

I frown. I was so consumed in overthinking that I didn't notice when my dad came back. There's no one in my sight, and after a brief moment I realize they must be in the kitchen.

"Quiet down," my father replies as I try to step a little closer so I can hear them better. "No one will rat us out, trust me."

Rat them out? What are they talking about?

The curiosity takes over me and I descend one more step, sticking my back to the wall like my life is depending on it. No matter the topic of their conversation, I don't want to get caught eavesdropping on them.

"What are we going to do about the Youngs, then? They'll keep trying to get to Elainne."

Hearing my name makes me jolt. What's wrong with the Young family? I concentrate as much as I can, but both of them lower their voices, and I can only occasionally catch the low baritone of my father's voice.

I want to step a little closer, to try and hear more, but there aren't that many stairs left, and if I do so, I will be exposed. With curiosity making my heart race, I forget all about the water and slowly go back up the stairs, careful to stay as quiet as possible. It's not until I close the door of my room that I allow myself to take a deep breath.

What was all of that about? I think about the Young family again, but I can't figure it out. Chris's parents were nothing but nice to me in the hospital. Jia's tear stricken face still haunts me, and I slump onto my bed. Their son was gone for over a month, and I was probably their last hope, but I couldn't help them. I couldn't save their son. I still can't save him.

They'll keep trying to get to Elainne. I know nothing useful, so why would they do that?

But even more importantly, why would my parents worry about them?

CHAPTER 4

The pleasant smell of fresh food tickles my senses, waking me up from my slumber. I slowly blink, trying to adjust my eyes to the morning light, only to see my mom quietly closing the door of my room with one hand, while holding a tray full of food in another. When she sees I'm awake, she smiles and brings the tray to my bed.

"Morning," she says as she sits on the edge of my bed. "I didn't want to scare you. I brought you some breakfast."

I look at the food, and my mouth waters at the sight. There is a plate full of delicious-looking waffles and some fruit. I thank her, and she leans in and leaves a kiss on my forehead.

"Do you want to make some paper crafts with me later?" she asks me.

I think about it for a second. It's something I'm supposed to like, something familiar to me. Maybe if I do so, I will remember something; be a step closer to the truth.

"Sure. Is there anything in particular we'll be making?"

"Not really, unless you have something in mind." She gives a glance to the interior of my room and its bland, almost empty walls. "We could make something for your room, though. It wouldn't hurt to add some colors in it."

"Oh, of course," I reply after a minute of contemplating. "I don't really have a preference."

For a split second, I catch her melancholic gaze, but the moment is over before I have the time to soak it in. "I thought it might remind you of something, maybe refresh your memory."

I wonder what to say to that, but decide to change the topic in the end. "I'll come downstairs after I eat and get dressed."

"Sounds good. I'll be in the living room in the meantime." She nods quickly, before getting up from my bed and leaving the room.

As I promised her, I finish my breakfast quickly and head downstairs with the tray she brought me, now lighter of the food that was previously placed on it. I stop by the kitchen to leave all the dishes in the sink, impatient to join my mom in the living room.

Once I step inside, I find her on the couch, surrounded with a bunch of colorful papers, scissors, and tubes of glue. She looks completely in her element as she carefully cuts a piece of paper, her eyebrows furrowed in a concentrated expression.

I feel a prick of guilt when I look at her like that, because it's clear how much she likes art in any form. As a museum curator, she was surrounded by art all day, but she took a month-long leave from work so she could take care of me. Unlike her, my dad is a manager of one of our local stores, so he can't take such a long leave whenever he wishes to.

"Oh, you're here," she says when she finally notices me standing here and watching her. "What are you waiting for? Come here." She moves her art supplies, and then pats the freshly decluttered space on the couch.

I walk over to her and grab a baby pink sheet of paper from a small pile. She explains the process to me, and after a few minutes, I already have a couple of small stars laying in front of me. As it turns out, this isn't hard to make, so maybe not all hope is lost.

My hands pick up the pace on their own in no time, so I let my thoughts wander freely as I work with the paper. This feels like a perfect morning, and I wonder how many times we went through this same scenario in the past. I may not remember it, but it seems that my hands do. When I was in the hospital, Dr. Brennan—a psychiatrist who treated me—told me that the skills I had should stay intact despite my memory loss, and now I believe she was right, at least about this.

"We already have a lot of stars, do you want to try something else now?" Mom asks me, interrupting my thoughts.

I nod and move all the stars we made aside. She wants to teach me how to make origami, so I sit and carefully soak in all of her explanations. We decide to start with a simple cat, and after a lot of her guidance, I manage to make almost an exact replica of hers.

After the first cat, we make another one, then another one, and then another one, until we finally move on to the next animal. All of them demand a sharp eye for details, one which I don't possess, but Mom clearly does. She spots every mistake I make in an instant and corrects me before I have the chance to mess up even more.

"Okay, now fold it here..." she instructs me as I go, and with an occasional correction from her, I end up with a beautiful, bright yellow butterfly. "Great job. You can put this one somewhere in your room. It's pretty, and butterflies symbolize rebirth."

I let out a surprised hum. "Really?"

"Yeah. They're beautiful little creatures. Do you want to make something else?"

"Sure, I think we've already made enough animals."

She smiles upon hearing my words. "Great. Can you pass me that red paper, please?"

I grab the paper, and something in me freezes. Red paper. The thought seems crazy, but I cling to her words, feeling the entire left side of my body flaring up as if it's set on fire.

The mysterious r. p. could be anything. For all I know, it could be a person as well. It could be so many different objects.

But what if it's as simple as a piece of red paper?

"Honey, are you okay?" My mom brushes a strand of hair out of my face, and I realize I've been staring at one spot on the floor for a few seconds.

"Yeah, yeah, just got a bit dizzy for a second, but I'm fine now," I try my best to brush it off. I don't know why I avoid telling anyone about the tattoo, but whenever I want to say something, I end up biting my tongue instead.

"Do you want to go to your room and rest? We can continue another day."

I contemplate. Do I want to go upstairs and stay alone with my thoughts? Realizing I have nothing better to do anyways, I agree. Mom helps me get back to my room, and then goes downstairs to make lunch. I didn't notice how quickly time flew by, so I'm surprised when I look at the clock and see it's already noon.

Once I successfully bury myself in the blankets, I observe my room. One word is enough to describe it: dull. Despite the addition of a yellow origami butterfly that's now resting on my desk, everything's the same as it used to be when I came back home. I don't remember seeing any red papers here, but maybe I just didn't look carefully enough. After all, it's easy to oversee something if I don't know I should be looking out for it.

Just yesterday I was thinking about the tattoo again, and I was convinced that r. p. is something that would take me ages to find, almost like an invisible entity that keeps slipping from my grasp. But maybe it doesn't have to be so complicated.

Of course, I might be wrong. It feels too easy to be true, and I might not even find anything noteworthy, but the least I can do is try. Besides, it's not like I have a lot to do instead.

A gentle knock on the door breaks the silence inside the room. "Elainne?" It's Mom, and I wonder why she's back so quickly.

"Yes?" Despite my permission, she doesn't even open the door.

"I'm going to run to the store to get some ingredients. I'll be back soon in case you need anything."

"Got it!" I only hear her footsteps as she goes back down the hallway. Maybe this is the chance I need.

I wait a few minutes, until I'm sure she's really gone. Then I rise from underneath the blankets and start circling around the room.

The desk sounds like the most reasonable place to begin my search, so I approach it carefully and open the drawer. This is the second time I'm doing this since I came back home, and when I've done it for the first time, I closed it after just a few glimpses. Needless to say, the inside of the drawer was in chaos.

In comparison to that, the surface of the desk seems pretty tidy despite everything that's laying on top of it. I make enough space for me to put all the contents of my drawer and begin the sorting. First I move the stationery aside, putting it all on one pile, then put the papers on the other, and make a third pile for everything else. When the entire drawer is empty, I go through the papers one by one.

The first thing I notice is that I really loved to write random notes. I'm not sure what half of them mean. Some of them have a single word written on them, some have dates and times—possibly of exams, or perhaps appointments—and some look like fragments of notes torn out of the notebook. There are a few colored paper notes, but none of them are red.

I sigh and focus my gaze on a now-empty drawer, as if staring at it will give me an idea of what to do next. I inspect its interior, but it looks just like any normal drawer—a plain, wood-like look, decorated only by some traces of pen ink on the sides that were probably left by accident. Well, it was worth a try.

Defeated, I decide to put everything back into the drawer. One by one, the stationery and other items are inside once again, and all that's left are the old notes. I grab the little pile with both of my hands, but a few slips of paper escape my grasp and fall onto the floor.

I put the rest into the drawer and crouch down to pick them up with a grunt. Once I collect them all, I jerk back to my feet, but my head collides with the sharp edge of the drawer.

Wincing, I stay on the floor and rub the back of my head. Hello, new headache.

"Stupid drawer!" I mutter under my breath and glare at its traitorous bottom.

And that's when I notice it—a small piece of red string tucked between the bottom and front boards.

It's perfectly hidden by the wider rim of the drawer's front board, so I doubt I'd spot it if I was looking from a different angle. Maybe I do have a sharp eye for details, after all. I carefully take it between my fingers and try to pluck it out, but instead, the entire board gives in and something red flutters before my eyes.

I close my eyes instantly, preparing for a crashing sound of the drawer's contents hitting the floor, but it doesn't come. With a deep breath, I slowly open my eyes and realize I'm still holding the string.

Surprised, I stare at the thing in my hands. The string is glued tightly to a thin wooden board that fits into the bottom of the drawer perfectly. I try to move the board, but it doesn't budge, so it must be fixed to the back of the drawer, the only part that I can't reach.

I just found a secret compartment.

Ecstatic, I move my gaze to the floor, and sure enough, a piece of red paper lies next to me.

"1984 G. O."

I pick up the paper to examine the words on it. More initials? Something about this is familiar, but I cannot remember what exactly. I turn the paper around, but I only find some doodles and a small "R3D" written in the corner.

Very confused, I put the paper on my desk and try to put the board back into its place. It takes me a few tries, but eventually it sticks, and I make sure that the string is safely hidden, just like it was when I first noticed it.

As I get back to my feet, I can't help but wonder how did that thing even end up here. Someone must've put it in place, but was that someone me?

I shift my focus back onto the paper. There's so many different things written on it, but I can't decipher anything. I hurriedly bury it underneath all the other notes and stationery and as I close the drawer, it suddenly clicks to me why the first note is familiar.

I walk over to the bookshelf, looking for a particular book. When I finally spot it, I pull it out and examine its front cover. It's called 1984, and the author's name is George Orwell, which fits the cryptic note perfectly. There's some familiar sensation as I'm holding the book, but I can't quite put my finger on what it is. It's clear that I've read it before, maybe even more than once. It seems to be very well kept, but it still has the charm of a book that's been opened times and times before.

"Elainne! I'm back!" I hear the shouts from downstairs, and the sudden breaking of silence almost makes me drop the book. I put it back on the bookshelf for now and make sure everything else is exactly how it used to be, then swiftly get into my bed again.

My thoughts race wildly as I start coming up with new theories. At first, I didn't believe I'd find something—not really—but I still wanted to try. And now, I found a secret compartment and a very mysterious note by pure luck. I'm not sure if it means anything at all, but the secrecy intrigues me regardless. Would anyone even think of looking for a secret compartment at the bottom of the drawer? I certainly wouldn't.

With a frustrated sigh, I wrap up the blankets tighter around me. Maybe I'm still not on the right track, but at least I have a book that might give me some answers.

Chapter 5

As much as I want to satisfy my curiosity and start reading 1984 right away, I decide to give it a day and get some good sleep first. After all, I had enough headaches for one day.

When I wake up the next morning, I stretch my muscles, and then a knock on the door interrupts me.

"Yes?" I call, already guessing who's on the other side.

I'm not surprised when my mother opens the door, holding a tray filled with food, just like she did yesterday.

"Oh, you're awake."

I accept the tray from her with a yawn. "I just woke up a minute ago."

"Great. Guess what I found?" she changes the topic, and I look at her in confusion.

"What?" I mumble out, looking at my food.

"Your photo album! I've been looking for that one for days, but I couldn't find it anywhere. I finally thought of looking on the one shelf where I thought it definitely wouldn't be, and there it was."

I put a piece of pancake into my mouth and slowly chew as she talks. "That's cool," I say with a nod when she finishes.

She clasps her hands together with an excited smile. "Do you want to take a look at it together later?"

"Oh, sure. I'll be there when I'm done eating." She doesn't argue against it and quickly leaves me to eat in peace. Curiosity takes over me, so I try to finish my plate as soon as I can so I'll take a look at the photos.

Once I'm downstairs, I found my mom in the living room with an album in her lap, flipping through the pictures.

"Is that the one?" I ask her.

She gives me a quick nod and pats the seat next to her. "I already looked at all the pictures earlier, but I started looking again. Don't worry, though, we'll start from the beginning."

As I sit down next to her, she goes back to the very first page, and the picture of a sleeping baby greets me. The small creature is wrapped into a baby pink blanket and wears a small cap, making its face the only visible feature on the photo.

"This was the first picture of you. You were just a day old here." Dazed, I don't know what else to say, so I just nod in response.

As we go through the album, the baby slowly turns into a toddler, and then into a smiling little girl. Sometimes she's alone in the pictures, and sometimes she's accompanied by her parents, the younger versions of the people I know today. I realize I must've been a happy child, and the realization leaves a bitter taste in my mouth.

My parents already told me lots of stories from my child-hood, and Mom only adds to them as she flips through the pages, but despite that, I don't feel like that child was actu-ally me. I only have the stories they tell me; not the actual memories of those things happening.

Once again, I'm consumed by guilt. All my parents want me is to recover, and I feel like I'm letting them down by not regaining any memories just yet. But I cling to the last bit of hope I have now—the book that's waiting for me upstairs.

Now that I've remembered all about my yesterday's discov-ery, I can't wait to see the last page of the album so I could run back to my room and start reading, but I force myself to be patient and sit through the illustrated gradient of my childhood.

I anticipate the look of disappointment on my mother's face when I tell her I don't recall any of the stories she told me. However, in an attempt to console her, I say that I enjoyed hearing about them before I awkwardly retreat to my room.

As soon as I close the door behind me, I go to the bookshelf, find the book in question, and return to my bed with it. I already examined its outside yesterday, but I am yet to look inside. As it turns out, my previous predictions are true, because the numerous annotations and notes inside imply that I've read it multiple times already.

I start reading, and the first one of them soon catches my eye. It's almost at the very beginning of the book, and the passage is written in capitalized letters.

"WAR IS PEACEFREEDOM IS SLAVERYIGNORANCE IS STRENGTH"

I pause for a second, thinking about the words. It's a twisted slogan of the Party, and it looks like I already had some thoughts on it before. From those few lines, an arrow is drawn with a pencil, and I notice my crumpled handwriting on the margin that says, "that's what they want you to believe".

There are others like that one, resembling the Party's slogans, and I find myself feeling dreadful from the very first pages. Soon enough, I become so endorsed in the book that I barely notice a knock on my door. This time, my mom opens them without my answer. "Hey, the lunch is ready."

Already? Slightly dazed, I look at the clock and notice that it's already way past noon. I didn't check the time when I returned to my room, but it must've been around an hour since I started reading, and I'm surprised that there's no annoying headaches now.

"What are you reading? You didn't even hear when I was knocking." she asks when she noticed the book in my lap. Her eyebrows furrow as she closes the door behind her and approaches my bed.

"Oh, sorry, I got a little carried away. It's a book I used to read for school," I waste no time saying. "I found some notes about it in one of my notebooks, so I was curious. I wanted to read it and see if it would look familiar." Of course, that was a lie, although I wonder if I really learned about this book in school before, or if I simply read it for my own enjoyment.

She seems satisfied with my answer, and I put the book aside for now. "Alright, but just make sure not to read too much. If you feel like a headache is starting, better leave the book for later, okay? There's no rush." Gently leaning in, she kisses my forehead. Her breath tickles my skin, but I feel warmth when she hugs me.

"I know," I murmur, still in her arms. "I didn't read too much anyways, I'll probably stop soon."

"Alright," she whispers, "just take care of yourself." She releases me and then pinches my cheek. "And don't forget to come to eat."

"I'll be right there," I reply as she leaves my room, but despite saying that, I pick up the book again. I just turned the new page when she came in, so I decide to read until the end, and then go back downstairs. Just when I reach the bottom, I see a passage that grabs my attention.

"The past, he reflected, had not merely been altered, it had been actually destroyed. For how could you establish even the most obvious fact when there existed no record outside your own memory?"

What catches my eye is the red pen in which the passage is marked, as well as another scribbled note on the margins: "too bad they didn't have any flash drives :/"

Red.

A flash drive. Maybe what I need is a flash drive.

Chapter 6

Despite my curiosity, it takes me a couple of days to finish the book. Soon after finding the comment about the flash drive, another interesting passage pops up. While the author describes the way Winston destroys the evidence of being ordered to alter the truth, as well as his own notes about it, a comment on the margin says, "be careful of what you're writing down ;)".

Whether it's really meant to be a warning or not, I take it as a sign that I shouldn't write down any clues I find in the book, so—ironically enough—I have to rely on my memory for those.

As I read, I notice a lot of passages that the past me tried to highlight, some of them with their own little comments on the side.

"Everything faded into mist. The past was erased, the erasure was forgotten, the lie became truth." The quote is accompanied by an ominous, "one should never believe everything that is served to them".

"For the first time he perceived that if you want to keep a secret you must also hide it from yourself." This line appeared towards the end of the book, followed with an ambiguous "hide it where no one can see it".

They all seem to tell me something, warning me of the danger that might be lurking around me. I notice a lot of passages and lines that are underlined and simply highlighted with exclamation marks. I flip through the book, trying to put them all together.

"It was true that he had no memories of anything greatly different."

Despite the original passage talking about how Winston's surroundings have always been the same, for as long as he could remember, I oddly relate to it as well. The irony is hard to miss, because I have no memories of a different life either.

"To do anything that suggested a taste for solitude, even to go for a walk by yourself, was always slightly dangerous."

"A Party member lives from birth to death under the eye of the Thought Police. Even when he is alone he can never be sure that he is alone."

There are some other marked quotes that seem to have a similar theme to these ones, and I can't help but try to imagine how scary it must be to live that way—constantly watched over by someone, not being able to have any time for yourself, stripped of any privacy.

"Everything depends on yourself."

I go back and forth between the quotes, trying to figure out if I may have misunderstood something. The crumpled hand-writing on the margins matches the one from my notebooks, but it doesn't tell me much more than that.

When all the quotes are put together, they paint quite a concerning story. They look like something that only a very lonely and scared person would relate to, so I wonder what happened to make the past me mark those things as impor-tant.

Was I already aware that someone wished me harm before I was kidnapped, which made them so significant? And if that was really the case, then who could've it been?

I'm still missing many pieces of the puzzle, but luckily for me, the quotes aren't the only clues in the book. There are some smaller ones, just bits and pieces and scattered words underlined in different ways.

I easily separate them into two groups. The first ones are all in close proximity, hidden in the early parts of the book. I have "memory holes", "document", "books", and "photographs", all marked with a single straight line underneath them.

The others are harder to find since they're scattered throughout the rest of the book, but a wavy line they're marked with clearly sets them apart: "vast land spaces", "four", "the rocks", "Look at the stars!", "surface of water", and "flame".

While the first ones point at something concrete, the second group leaves me confused. They are clearly clues about something, but I don't know what just yet. I finally decide to let it go for now and put the book back in its place on the bookshelf. I know I can't remember everything I found, and since writing things down isn't an option, I mark the pages where all the clues appear, because I'll definitely be revisiting them often.

With my mood significantly grimmer, I open my desk drawer and find the red piece of paper that I hid at the bottom. The first side is now clear as day to me; after all of this, I see I was right about 1984, but now it's turn for the other side to trouble me.

No matter how much I think about it, I still don't know what the "R3D" is about. I already figured that it must be pointing to the color red, which seems to be a common theme between all the clues, but why is it written in such a way?

I leave that question aside for now and focus on the drawings. They aren't anything special, just some amateur doodles, but I can't help but wonder if they have their own meaning too. A white dove, little crescent moon, a question mark, small scythe, a skull, a trident, and something that looks like a droplet, or a tear; they're scattered across the tiny piece of paper, challenging me to solve their mystery.

A hollow ping of a message notification breaks my focused gaze. I put the red paper back and quickly take my phone. When my screen lights up, I see that I have a text message from Jane.

'I was thinking of coming over with some of our friends tomorrow afternoon to visit you. Let me know if that works for you x'

As I read the message, I realize I've completely forgotten about Jane. Lately, the only thing I've been thinking about are the cryptic clues the past me left behind. It's funny how easily someone can trap themself inside their own mind and forget about the outside world. I've been stuck in this little bubble, cushioned by the comfort of my bedroom.

I look at the screen again, and her words remind me of the quotes I previously marked in 1984. In one of them, Winston was talking about using the word "friend", and I marked that part, saying "be careful of who you're calling a friend" beside it.

If there's a specific person that note was referring to, then Jane might have some answers for me.

With my thoughts heading in that direction, I think about Chris again. As our classmate and friend, Jane should at least help me shine some light on my relationship with him, as well as our relationships with others. I still don't understand why the two of us were the targets, but if I want to solve this mystery, I'll have to find out.

CHAPTER 7

"**S**weetie, your friends are here," Mom says from the other side of the door and I sigh, realizing I'll have to go downstairs and leave my bubble for a while.

When I enter the living room, I see three girls sitting on the couch. They look up at me, and the one in the middle waves at me with a smile on her face.

"Elainne! Hi! It's so good to see you." Jane gets on her feet and comes to greet me. I don't expect a hug from her, but I awkwardly wrap my hands around her, returning it. When she releases me, she points to the two girls still seated on the couch. "These two are Charlotte Davidson and Naomi Samson." Since she doesn't say anything else about them, I assume they're my old classmates as well. "I wanted to come and see you, but they missed you too, so we decided to pay you a visit together."

When she finally stops talking, I sit in an armchair next to the couch, while she takes her previous spot. I sneak a few glances at Charlotte and Naomi. Their faces feel brand new to me, like I've never seen them before. If any other classmates stopped by, would I remember them, or would they be brand new people to me too?

"Only the three of us are here now," Jane says, "but everyone in school misses you so much. We all hope you'll feel better soon and come back."

The other two nod, confirming Jane's statement, but something about it reminds me of my "be careful of who you're calling a friend" note from 1984. Now that I think about it, it makes me wonder. The girls seem friendly, but almost too friendly to me. Their smiles and enthusiasm look exaggerated to the point where I'm starting to doubt things again.

If there's anything the book made clear so far, it's that my life surely isn't as perfect as it looks.

I manage to put a polite smile on my face. "Can you tell me more about them?"

"Our classmates? Of course! Don't worry, that's what we're here for." Her words make it sound like she's only here for gossip, and truly, that seems to be the only thing on her mind.

She tells me about our other classmates, revealing the latest dramas and other people's relationships, but the names she tosses around get lost in my mind as soon as she says them. Charlotte and Naomi aren't any better, mainly letting Jane talk and only occasionally adding to the gossip.

For a second, I consider running out of the room and just leaving them on the couch. I don't need to know about the relationship status of every person in our school. I need something that might actually be helpful to me.

"What about Chris?" I finally take my chance to ask when she stops to catch her breath.

"Chris?" she asks dumbfounded.

"Yeah, the guy who was kidnapped with me. What can you tell me about him?"

The three of them glance at each other awkwardly, as if they're unsure what to say.

"Well," Naomi starts, "we don't really know a lot about him. He was always a very shy and a bit antisocial guy. He mostly hung out with you, actually."

Somehow, that surprises me. It doesn't fit the impression I previously had, although I'm not even sure if that was the right one. His parents described him as a lovely child, but they never said anything about his friends.

I let them continue, tuning them out entirely. They might've noticed my change in mood, because soon they awkwardly look at the time and say they'll have to take their leave. I can't help but think to myself how they sure left fast for people who claimed they missed me a lot.

I happily retreat to my room right after they leave, pondering over everything they told me. Most of the information already dissipated, gone from my mind without a trace. But the one thing they said about Chris, however little, leaves me thinking. I grab the origami butterfly from my nightstand and twist it around in my fingers, careful not to mess up any loose folds.

Even after all this time, I'm not sure what to think about Chris. He's like an unanswered question lingering at the back of my mind. I've been trying to solve this mystery because he might be somewhere out there, waiting for my help, but I just kept finding more and more questions without an answer. Or am I like this origami, so tangled up in this mess that there's no possible way to go back to the start?

The butterfly gives me no reply, so I just keep laying in my bed until I hear my dad come back home. I look at the clock and see it's almost dinnertime, so I go back downstairs to greet him.

He's in the living room, sitting on the couch, but when he sees me, he pats the spot next to him, beckoning me to come closer. "Hey, sweetie. How was your day?" he asks as I sit down.

"Fine," I mutter. "Some friends from school stopped by and paid me a visit."

"Oh, really? Which ones?"

I tell him their names and he nods with a smile. "That's nice. How are the headaches?"

"It's getting better, I rarely have them nowadays." What I say is completely true. They have been very generous to me lately, rarely haunting me anymore. In fact, ever since I started reading 1984 and hunting down my own clues they eased down, as if they knew that was something really important to me, something I needed to push through no matter what.

I try to think of what to say in return, so I ask him about his work. "Oh, it was fine, I just had to stay overtime because we got a new delivery today and storage room was a mess," he says as he lazily scratches his ear, and then yawns, showing how tired he is.

Just when I'm about to reply, Mom calls us over to the dining room. Unlike the first time I returned home, there's no more awkward atmosphere while we eat. Instead, we chat casually, and they even talk about some of my childhood memories.

"...and then you ran over to me, but you didn't cry at all, you just stared at me and said 'Daddy, this bike is evil.' with a most adorable serious expression I've ever seen." We all laugh as dad finishes the story of my first attempt to ride a bike when I was a child.

I stare at my plate, thinking about all those memories I've lost. Now, the only ones I can rely on to help me recall them are my parents. Even if I gather every single person I've interacted with throughout my life, they could only tell me so much. What if there's a part of me that will always be lost, leaving a gaping hole in the puzzle of my life?

Reluctantly, I remember the conversation I overheard a few days ago. Even if my parents told me everything, could I really trust them? I look at both of them, carrying on with their conversation. The entire night feels perfect, like something is finally going right after all this time, but how much of that perfect picture is real?

Maybe I just misunderstood them. Maybe they didn't mean anything bad. Maybe the Youngs are truly the bad guys, and they just wanted to protect me. I can't help but feel like there's danger looming over me and that there's somebody who wishes me harm, but I can't figure out who that might be.

I'm stuck in the sea of "what if"s once again, and I can't discern the truth. But if I want to get all my memories back and try to save Chris, I'll have to do it before it's too late.

Chapter 8

W ith nothing better to do, I spend my days trying to solve the mystery behind the "R3D" note and the weird scribbles accompanying it. By now, I'm already convinced that they have their own meaning too. Since I couldn't figure it out, I read 1984 again, trying to see if there are any hints that I might've missed, but there are none.

I sigh, looking at my bookshelf, as if it's going to give me an answer. In the past few days, I didn't have the chance to examine the house more carefully and look for any other clues, so I'm still stuck in a status quo.

Before I put the book back, I decide to reorganize the entire bookshelf. It looks like a mess with the books placed anywhere, without a rule or order. That's been bothering me for a while, but now I finally decide to do it and distract myself from the clues.

I sit on the floor, examining the books. After I think of multiple options, I decide to organize them by colors. I carefully split them all into different piles, and then start placing them back on the bookshelf. If only I could sort out my thoughts as easily as I sorted out these books.

But then, when I get to the red pile, something catches my eye. I look at the books and read all the descriptions on the back. Then, as if the floor beneath me became scorching hot, I jump up and run to my desk. It doesn't take me too long to find the red note that I hid inside the drawer. I go back to the other side of the room with it and analyze the scribbles.

Some of them match the books.

I flip through each one, trying to see if there are any clues in them, but I only find numbers at the back, written with a red pen. That's it.

I put them next to each other, starting with the book number one, and finishing the row with book number seven. I compare them one by one, trying to find the connections.

Scythe. A little scythe is on the paper, standing out as the most obvious connection. Dracula. What I thought might be a tear is probably supposed to represent a drop of blood. The Battle of the Labyrinth. A trident matches the one on the cover. Sisters Red. This one is harder to figure out, but the description mentions werewolves, so I connect it with the crescent moon. An Anonymous Girl. A question mark. Vicious. It takes me a while, but I realize that one's connected with the skull drawing. Evernight. There's only one scribble left, the one of the dove. At first, I can't find the connection, but all the other books fit, and this one also bears a number on the back, so I realize they must have a connection.

When I'm done with the scribbles, I think about the last clue, the last piece of the puzzle. R3D. If it's on the same side of the note as the pictures, then it must be connected to these books somehow.

My mind races, fueled by the newest discovery. If the letter E is replaced with a number, then are the letters from the books supposed to be replaced with numbers too? Since E looks similar to 3, I try that method, searching for the lookalike numbers, but I don't get too far.

"Alright, if it's not that, then what?" I mutter to myself as my eyes dance back and forth between the books in front of me. A letter replaced with a number...

After thinking it through for a while, I come up with only two options, but none of them seem related to the way R3D is written. I take out the first letter of every book's name, then replace every second letter with the number on the back of that book, until I get something that resembles a code.

S2T4A6E

Still hesitant, I start the same process again, but this time I replace those letters with their numbers in the alphabet.

S4T19A22E

When I look at the codes, both seem... correct to me, but I have no idea if they'll actually work. Work for what? It looks like a random mix of letters and numbers, but it's chosen carefully, so it must have its purpose. And that purpose is probably a password for something.

I quickly get on my feet again and rush to my desk, where the only thing requiring a password now collects dust. When I tried to use my laptop before, it needed a password to be unlocked, and just like everything else, I didn't know what it was.

Luckily for me, its battery is still working properly, and I watch in anticipation as the screen lights up. Soon enough, the little password box pops up, and I type in the first code.

WRONG PASSWORD

"Okay, please be the second one," I whisper as I anxiously type the second code, although a part of me expects me to be wrong again.

But the display changes, and I see the desktop.

I stare in disbelief, blinking slowly to make sure that what I'm seeing is not an illusion. The approach I took was completely unrelated to the note, but it actually worked.

After I snap back out of it, I quickly go through the files, looking for anything that could help, but there's nothing on it. Taking a deep breath, I try once again, but the laptop barely has anything on it. On a second thought, I notice that even the desktop background shows a green field with a clear blue sky. Nothing personal. Nothing that could help me.

I blink twice, completely dumbfounded. This was something that belonged to me. I can see some traces in there, a couple of documents for school assignments and some basic things here and there, but it doesn't feel mine. In fact, it feels like I've reached a dead end. If the password fit, that must mean the laptop is part of the solution as well, but how can it be so if there's nothing on it now?

Or was there even anything to begin with?

The thought strikes me out of nowhere. Of course. After all, what I ultimately need is a flash drive. But even if I find it, I need to plug it into another device to see whatever it is that it contains. If the flash drive has everything I need, then I probably didn't even need any other personal files here.

Breathe, Elainne. Just breathe. Maybe there's still some hope for this. But if I don't find the flash drive, then this discovery is completely in vain, so I turn off my laptop, finish reorganizing the bookshelf, and then go back to thinking.

Chapter 9

E ver since I found the password for my laptop, I've been eager to investigate more and try to find the flash drive, but I was rarely left all alone in the house. The opportunity doesn't come until two days later, when mom comes into my room and tells me she'll need to head out.

"Your dad just called me. I'm not sure what happened, but he told me there's been some mess at the store, so he needs me to bring him a new shirt. I'll head out for a bit, would you be fine on your own?"

I barely hide my excitement. "Yes, of course. Say hi to him from me."

"Will do!" she shouts, already back in the hallway. I tiptoe to the window and peek through it, watching as she leaves the driveway. The second she's out of reach, I take a deep breath, reassessing the clues I have so far.

Among the two groups, one seems to have a common theme. Memory holes probably refers to my missing memories, while I'm pretty sure that books was pointing at 1984 and the red books that brought me to my laptop's password. Document is the one I don't fully understand yet, but there might be a document on the flash drive.

I pause and mull over the last one. Photographs. It's the only clue I have for now, no matter how weak.

I decide to start from the one photograph I have in my room. It shows a little version of me in our backyard, with both of my parents-who look slightly younger than now-by my side. I grab its simple white frame and pick it up from my nightstand. The picture itself doesn't arouse any suspicion in me, and even inspecting the frame and the back of the picture doesn't give me any results.

Instead of sulking, I only inhale deeply and put it back in its place. That is a good sign. The past me clearly decided to make this hunt as complicated as possible, so finding any clues from this would feel wrong.

I hop out of my bed and leave my room. Despite being alone in the house, I tiptoe my way down the stairs, but I pause midway through.

For the first time since I came back home, I stop to inspect the pictures on the wall more closely. I never paid them much attention before, giving them a passing glance every now and then. The only thing I know is that they're pictures of me and my family, but that's about it.

Soon enough, I realize that was a big mistake.

The first thing I notice is that there's four of them. Four. It already fits one of the clues, although that's the most vague one I have, so the number may not mean anything here.

The first picture in the row shows me and my mom standing on what appears to be a cliff. Behind us is a wide area of layered rocks, and our expressions are unclear, shadowed by sunglasses and hats. The bottom right corner of the picture says Grand Canyon. If I compare this to my clues, vast land spaces and the rocks seem to fit this picture.

The next one shows a slightly younger me sitting in front of a tent with dad. A huge grin is plastered over my face and his arm is resting on my shoulder. The starry night sky looms above us, and there's a small bonfire nearby. Look at the stars! Flame. I mentally cross off other clues one by one before I move on to the next picture.

This one shows the three of us on the couch in the living room. I sit between my parents, right in the middle of the couch, with only a hint of a smile on my face and my hands resting on the couch cushion underneath me. Weirdly enough, no clues fit this one. There is only one clue left, and it fits the last picture in the row.

Surface of water. The photograph shows me standing on a beach, dressed in a purple one-piece swimsuit. My bare feet are covered in sand, while the beautiful blue sea stretches out everywhere behind me.

Three pictures fit perfectly well with the second group of clues I had, but one of them doesn't. I carefully grab its frame and remove it from the wall, inspecting it so closely that my nose almost touches the glass. Not finding anything suspicious on the picture, I turn it over and remove the back cover, trying to see if there's anything written on the back of the picture.

Nothing.

Not even a single word or number, anything to show me that these pictures are really the right place to look at. Faced with the sudden block on the road, I put the photograph back on the wall, and then glance back and forth between them.

Then the realization hits me, and I run to the living room.

Please, let me be right about this one. Please...

I kneel in front of the couch and try to lift the middle cushion. At first it doesn't budge, but slowly, it begins to move inch by inch, until I'm able to look at the bottom of it.

And I see a small lump at the back, covered in silvery duct tape.

I squeeze my hand inside and remove the tape with lightning speed, but still careful not to damage the couch. Just as I predicted, a small flash drive is hiding inside.

A shocked laugh breaks out of me. Great job, Elainne. I crumple on the floor in disbelief, gripping the flash drive like my life depends on it.

I should've figured it out sooner, but the third picture was the only one showing the inside of the house. The other clues were there to point at the rest of the pictures, because the lack of hints for the third one was supposed to be a hint in itself.

My head is dizzy from the adrenaline, but I force myself to get back on my feet and put the couch cushion back into its place, then head back to my room. As I pass the four pictures next to the stairs, I fix their frames, making sure they look the same as they did before I arrived.

As soon as I get back inside my room, I take my laptop and throw myself on the bed. I type in the password, and within seconds, the laptop is unlocked, and the flash drive is already inside of it.

The very last unanswered clue finally makes sense when I see a single document on the flash drive, titled if you forget. I shiver seeing the words that match those from my tattoo, and then click on the document.

The large title on the top says "if you forget", and I see multiple numbered points underneath it. This is it. There's no turning back now. With a final tremble, I take a fre deep breaths and start reading.

1. If you're reading this, it must mean you've lost your memory and you followed the clues all the way to the flash drive (if all of the clues were still intact)

2. Your name is Elainne Winfield

I stop for a second and pause, warding off my anxiety. For now, everything makes sense. Reassured, I move forward, but I quickly realize I shouldn't relax just yet.

3. You made this document because you suffer from athazagoraphobia. That's the fear of memory loss. This is the most reliable method, because no one else can be trusted enough.

That's it? I look at the words once again as if they'll change under my scrutinizing gaze. With a sigh of defeat, I can't help but think how that isn't what I expected. I don't remember anything about this fear, but it seems that it was strong enough to push me to do something like this.

4. YOUR FAMILY IS LYING TO YOU. If they're still around and they're treating you nice, DON'T FALL FOR IT. They only want you to stay by their side so they could control you. Don't trust a word they say.

I freeze upon seeing the next point. A part of me is rendered speechless, while the other part is not surprised at all. No matter how much I wanted to, I never completely trusted them, but was it really this bad?

5. They're the biggest narcissists you've ever met. They always tried to manipulate you into thinking you're nothing without them so they would keep you by their side and turn you into a mini copy of them to make themselves feel better. They love to watch over you at all times and control your movements and contacts. You suspected they might've even hacked your devices and listened to your phone conversa-

tions, but you never had solid proof for that so it was nothing more than a suspicion.

I sit in the library, my hands typing vigorously on the keyboard. I turn around to look behind myself before continuing. It's alright, there's no one else in the room just yet, and it's not very likely that they'll find a way to spy on me even here. As long as I hide this flash drive well, I'll probably be safe...

The memory comes out of nowhere, making my breathing faster and more erratic, so I waste no time in reading further.

6. You don't have a lot of friends in high school. Most of the people usually avoid you and don't want to talk to you. You tend to be distrustful of most people, so you hardly make any new friends.

7. You do have one good friend though. His name is Christian Young, but you usually call him Chris. You never told your parents about him, because you feared they would somehow make you stop hanging out with him.

Chris's cheerful face slowly comes into focus as the ripples of another memory become clearer in my mind.

We're sitting on a bench in the old park behind our high school. I managed to steal a bit of time before going home, just so I could sit here and pretend that everything in my life is alright.

I look at the boy next to me. Shy rays of October sun are illuminating his dark hair, but he doesn't notice that as he rummages through his backpack. He then takes out two candy bars and offers one of them to me.

All of a sudden, I feel a weird sense of peace I haven't felt in a long time. I got used to spending time by myself, and even when I'd hang out with some other friends, it never felt sincere enough. But Chris is too nice and straightforward for faking anything. Maybe I'm so in the wrong, but I feel like for the first time in my life, I have a true, real friend.

8. Jane Kinsley is one of the worst girls in your school. You used to be friends in middle school, but when high school started, you two met Chris and she had a crush on him. Since you and Chris quickly became friends, she wanted you to stay away from him, claiming he had a crush on you. You refused, and even though she quickly replaced that crush with a new one, you haven't been talking ever since. You usually avoid each other as much as you can. One time, she tried to spread some rumors about you two, but it never worked out for her. Pretty sure she talks trash about her "best friends" behind their backs too.

"I'm telling you, he has a crush on you! I need you to stay away from him." Jane crossed her arms, with her signature pout on her face. For some reason, she was convinced Chris had a crush on me, and she wouldn't stop bringing it up any chance she had.

"Why would I do that?" I look at Jane, completely bewildered. "We're already friends, and he's a nice guy, am I supposed to dump him just because of a crush you'll get over in a few weeks?"

9. Chris is the only one who knew something about your family situation, and he even offered to help you escape from them. If you're reading this, it means that the plan probably didn't work out.

"Hey, don't worry," Chris whispers into my ear as he hugs me. "You're not alone. We'll figure something out, okay? Have you considered just... I don't know, running away from them? Maybe I could help you hide at my place for a while. I'm sure my parents would understand if we told them what's going on."

10. You got the tattoo in late January of your senior year of high school. You tried your best to keep it a secret so that your parents wouldn't find out about it.

11. 1984 is your favorite book ever since you had to read it for literature class. You were supposed to write an essay about the book, and in the end, the teacher complimented yours, saying it was the best in the entire class. You decided to put the clues there because you've always related to that book so much.

I read the book again, this time thinking of the specific spots I could highlight. I already had a vague idea of the plan before I started reading, so I might need to give it a few more reads to solidify everything. With my reading speed, this should be set up by the end of next week.

12. Red is your favorite color

13. When you were little, you wanted to be a policeman or a detective, but when you grew older, you wanted to become a lawyer. You hoped that going to college will finally give you a chance to put some distance between you and your parents and step out of their shadow, but they didn't allow you to go. Probably because they were afraid they won't be able to control you anymore.

"Most parents can't wait for their kids to go to college, so why am I not allowed to go?" I cry out. No matter what I said, it was never enough to convince them to let me leave.

"Because we say no. You're staying here."

14. The place you always wanted to visit is Rome

15. Your favorite animal is a turtle

My mind is racing, overwhelmed by the sudden wave of memories. They flood over me until my heart threatens to burst out of my chest.

No, no, no, no, no. I thought I was really smart cracking all of these riddles and hunting the clues around the house, but I've actually been so stupid this entire time. How could've I trusted them?

My memories keep coming back, and I imagine a huge pile of golden keys in front of me. I try to remember what happened that faithful night, but that part is still locked for me. I know they were somehow involved, but I can't remember how or what happened.

I nearly jump out of my bed when I hear a car outside. Despite my legs trembling, I walk over to the window, and freeze when I see Jasmine's car outside. Still dizzy, I remove the flash drive and turn off the laptop, putting it back into its previous place. I run into my bathroom and lock the door, then turn on the water in the shower. But instead of coming in, I slump to the floor, my grip on the flash drive not weakening for a second.

I almost manage to calm down my breathing, when a knock on the bathroom door makes me jolt again.

"El, are you in here?" The sound of her voice makes me sick, but I take another deep breath before replying.

"Yeah, I'm taking a shower!"

"Do you need anything?"

"No, I'm fine!"

"Alright."

Once I believe she's out of the room, I bring my knees to my chest and hug them tightly. Soon, a strangled cry escapes my lips, and I sob quietly, the tears flowing down my face like water in the shower beside me.

How could I be so stupid to believe in their lies? Even when I felt like something was wrong, like there is more to this perfect image than I could see, I'd look for any excuse to shut those thoughts out and pretend that everything's fine.

Not only did I deliberately put myself deep into danger, but I dragged someone else with me too.

There's one lonely feeling echoing inside my heart when I think of Chris. Shame. He was my only friend, and he even tried to help me, but I endangered his life and separated him from his family in return. Is that the right way to thank him for being by my side?

My tears only run faster when I think of his parents and their desperate, sad faces. I need to help them. I need to find out what they did to Chris.

I take a deep breath, letting the water in the background drown out my thoughts, until I come up with a plan.

I already hate myself for what I'm going to do, but that's the only choice I have. I still can't remember that night, but if I had to guess, I'd assume Chris is still alive and locked up somewhere. My parents aren't the type to kill someone for no reason, and if they ever find out I got some memories back, they could use him as a leverage against me, so they're most likely keeping him alive. I only need to pretend I still don't know anything and buy myself some time until I remember where he could be.

I try not to think of all the ways my plan could go wrong, because there's too many. I need to save Chris, and this is my only hope. This time, he might be the one running out of time.

Chapter 10

The road ahead of me is empty. I run through the pitch black night with only one destination in mind.

I need to get there quickly. I'm running out of time.

Just when I slowly start losing breath, I see the police station ahead of me, like a beacon of light in the endless darkness. I race towards it, desperate for help.

I run in, but there is only one person, and it's the one I want to see the least.

"Hello, Elainne." Theodore looks at me from a few feet away, his lips slowly curling in a twisted grin. He stands there menacingly, waiting for me to come closer.

"No..." I mutter, backing away. I turn around and think of sprinting back towards the entrance, but Jasmine is standing there, with a grin identical to his. I didn't see her when I was walking in. Was she always there? Or was she behind me the entire time?

"Let me go... Let me leave!" a cry escapes from my lips.

My head snaps around wildly as I analyze my surroundings, looking for an exit. There is none. The two of them lurch towards me, and as they get closer to me inch by inch, their faces grow more distorted. Their hands reach for me, and I scream.

I jerk from the bed, my heart racing inside my chest. I try to calm my breathing down and blink away the darkness.

Bed. Blankets. Pillows. I'm in my room. That was just a dream.

If it was any less weird, maybe I'd believe it's a piece of my memories, but I'm sure it's not. However, what surprises me the most isn't the dream itself, but the fact that I remembered it after waking.

I've had a lot of dreams since I came back to this house, but most of them would be gone as soon as I'd open my eyes. There's only one other that I remember, and it's the one where Chris's parents screamed at me to give them back their child.

I sigh, burying my face into my knees. Ever since the moment my memories started coming back to me, I felt like there was somebody watching me all the time, an invisible gaze drilling holes into the back of my mind. Even now, in the middle of the night, I cannot escape that feeling, and I doubt it was a stranger to me before my amnesia.

I roll over in my bed until the morning, when a ping from my phone tells me I have a text message. Unsurprisingly, it's from Jane, since she texted me again last night.

'I'll see if I'll be able to stop by next week'

I reply to her with nothing but "Sounds good :)" and can't help but laugh at the irony of the situation. Now that I remember what a rotten wrench she is, that's all her fakeness is—funny.

When she came over with Charlotte and Naomi the other day, they told me that I was more popular among people and had a lot of friends, while Chris was a shy and reserved guy that hung out only with me. That story sounds perfectly fine at first, but the longer I think about it, the more hilarious it becomes—because the truth is actually the opposite.

The document helped me clear out the fog in my head, so now I know what the truth really is, and it's nothing like what they said. Chris was always way friendlier than me, and a lot of people liked him because of it, but I only had him.

I can't figure out what's the point of their fake niceness or completely distorting the truth. None of them liked me before all of this happened, so pretending they did just to get onto my good side is ridiculous. Especially when I'd eventually remember what happened in the past.

Speaking of the past, as if on cue, Jasmine comes to ask me if I'm awake and remind me to get ready for my doctor's appointment. Luckily, she reminded me about it the day before, otherwise I would have no idea. I'm not in the mood to spend any more time with my parents, let alone have them drive me to the hospital, but I have no say in the matter, so I'm stuck sitting in the back seat of Theodore's car as he drives us to the hospital. He's trying to keep the conversation going, but without much success, since I'm way too deep in thought to fake my interest in whatever he's saying, shutting both of them entirely as I replay some of my old memories.

I don't even notice when we arrive, but Jasmine opens the door for me, and the action snaps me out of my thoughts.

"I know you're nervous about the appointment, but there's nothing to worry about. The doctor's just going to check how your body's doing and see if there's been any progress with the memories," she tells me when I get out of the car.

So they think I'm just nervous about the appointment. Idiots.

After we give our information to the nurse at the reception desk, she instructs us to the doctor's office. We don't have to wait for too long before heading inside, and the serious face of an older doctor greets me.

He talks to both me and my parents at first, asking about my condition since I was discharged from the hospital, and then asks me about my headaches and whether or not I remembered anything in the meantime.

Despite having a previously prepared answer, a wave of cold sweat washes over me. At first, I'm honest about my headaches since I don't remember having one in a while. But when the doctor asks me about my memories, I lie. I would've lied even if Jasmine and Theodore weren't there with me, but their presence adds to the sense of urgency, like lying is the only thing I'm allowed to do. I just say how I vaguely remember some things from my childhood that my parents told me about and leave it at that.

Seeing how there's not much progress with my memories, the doctor ends the appointment, telling us to come back next month. Hopefully, I won't be anywhere near them by then.

After we leave the doctor's office, my parents decide to stay focused on the topic, so they try to talk about my memories on our way back, which means I can't keep ignoring them no matter how much I want to. Jasmine suggests we try to find more photo albums and look at them together, blissfully unaware of all the memories that already came back to me.

It's not until they ask me if I have any ideas that I make a mistake. "I could check if there's anything in my laptop," I say, trying to sound casual. Of course, I already know there's nothing on it, so it would be a dead end for them.

"Oh? Did you remember the password for it?" Theodore asks me.

Elainne, you idiot.

"No, not yet. Is another way to unlock it and bypass the password somehow? I don't know, something like hacking into it, I guess?" I try to save myself from my slip-up, and at the same time test a suspicion that the document raised for me.

"I don't know," he replies. "There probably is one. With the way technology is advancing, I wouldn't be surprised, although I haven't heard of it." Almost carelessly, he scratches his ear when he finishes talking.

Now that a lot of my memories are back, I can't help but notice the gesture. He does that when he lies. I don't think he was ever aware that I knew of his little tic, but it's still funny to see how easily they've let their guards down now that they think I don't know anything. I try to recall another recent instance where he's done that, and I remember that night when we talked in the living room. If he lied about staying overtime at work, then… Then he must've gone to the place where they're keeping Chris. That's a good sign.

I already expected them to keep Chris alive and well, but what shocks me is how easily my doubts are confirmed. That was the reason why I didn't have any personal things in my laptop. Or my bedroom. Or the entire house.

Thanks to them, I got used to moving through life like a ghost, constantly hiding the true pieces of myself in fear they'll get to know me better and use that against me. I almost laugh when I think about the flash drive where I hid the document. Even that was made in the public library, in a place they had no control over. I remember wanting to hide it in my bedroom at first, but I gave up of that because they'd find it easily. Instead, I hid it underneath the couch, because they'd never expect something so mine there. And the bottom of the couch cushions is the last place someone would pay attention to, so I knew it would be safe there.

When I look back at my life, I was always sticking out like a sore thumb. Most people want to be seen and heard, to leave their mark on this world, while I've always stubbornly strived for the opposite. Maybe this is my fate, to disappear without a trace, even from my own mind.

But now that I've already fulfilled it and found my way back once, it's time for me to fight back.

Chapter 11

As the days pass by, I only feel more disgusted with my own plan. I know I don't have a better choice at the moment, but I hate every second of pretending I'm completely clueless.

As crazy as it sounds, a part of me wishes I never remembered who I was. I think about 1984 once again and the Party's slogan that says how ignorance is strength, and now I can't help but agree with it. Maybe ignorance would help me start from scratch.

The worst thing of all is that I'm not doing anything to save Chris. I still don't have any important memories related to the night they kidnapped us, and sitting here idly in hope I'll remember something feels like a waste of time. Not mine, but his.

A gentle knock on my door startles me. I take a deep breath before answering.

"Hey, what are you doing?" Jasmine asks as she opens the door of my room. Even though I was just sitting on my bed and staring at the wall until a moment ago, her words make me feel like a criminal; like I'm doing something I'm not supposed to.

"Oh, nothing much. Why?" I reply, trying to push my anxiety down.

She enters inside and I notice her hands are full of something. "Look what I've made!" It takes me a minute to figure out what exactly I'm looking at, but then I realize she's carrying lots of paper stars, just like the ones we made together a while ago. "I have more of these for you! Do you want to put them up together? You still haven't put up the ones we made before."

I think about that day she invited me to hang out with her and make some paper crafts. That same day, I found the red paper in my room, so I was mostly focused on investigating and accidentally kept putting off decorating. However, after I finally remembered some things, I was avoiding it on purpose, but now I feel like I'm not allowed to refuse her request.

"Cool, thanks. Let me just get the old ones first," I say casually, and then walk over to my desk. I slowly open the drawer—where I've previously put them—and try not to think about the red note that's hidden somewhere inside.

The real reason why I've been avoiding decorating my room is that I never wanted those decorations here in the first place. My parents didn't remove any personal belongings from my bedroom; I never had any to begin with. Apart from my clothes, books, and school supplies, nothing in this room was truly mine, and I preferred it that way. It always felt like a temporary thing to me, a place I hoped I'd escape someday because I never felt safe here. It wasn't a home to me—it was just the place I lived in.

I sneak a peek at the laptop on my desk while Jasmine isn't looking. They didn't wipe my laptop clean from any personal files and made it seem like it belonged to a stranger; I never even made it mine in the first place. The only thing I could trust with some real parts of myself was something that could be hidden more easily; something like a flash drive. If I didn't have it, I wouldn't have needed that laptop at all. It didn't mean anything to me, it only contributed to my ghost image.

But when the decorating is done and my wall is full of colorful paper stars, I realize I'm something even worse than a ghost. I'm their puppet. This is what Jasmine wanted, not me. They've always tried to turn me into a mini version of themselves that they could control as they wanted, and now that I've lost all my memories, they finally got the chance to regain their control over me and do that.

"Alright, we're all done! It really looks better now, doesn't it?" She clasps her hands together with a satisfied smile on her face.

I nod and agree weakly in hopes she'll leave me alone soon, and she does. After she's finally gone, I decide to take a shower and let the cold water wash out all of my grim thoughts. However, I'm quickly done, and I hastily hop out of the shower, wrapping a towel around my body. In the process, my fingers trace the edges of my tattoo for barely a second, but it's still on my mind when I get back to my room and open my closet, looking for some clothes to put on.

I comb through the rack and after a couple of minutes, I narrow my choice to only two shirts—a plain olive one, and a red one with a logo I don't recognize anymore. Unexpectedly, I lose my breath when an identical scene plays out in my head, as if I'm dragged back through time.

I stand in front of my closet barefoot, trying to decide which shirt to put on tonight. I go back and forth between a bright red one, and another, olive one.

Thinking how Chris will probably wait for me the entire night if I don't make up my mind quickly, I change my mind and take the third, black one.

*

We're sitting on the rusty swings in the abandoned park behind our school. Even though it's already late in the evening, we're not in a rush to go back to our homes. Well, I'm certainly not.

Laughter breaks out of me when Chris tells me the newest of his many lame jokes. It's not actually funny, but I know he's trying his best to cheer me up.

Our laughter echoes throughout the park, so I notice something's wrong a second too late. I look at Chris just in time to see his eyes go wide with shock as one hand clamps over my mouth, and another one over my eyes.

*

My whole world is shrouded in darkness. I try to blink it away, but I feel my eyelashes rubbing against a piece of fabric. Since my sight isn't of much use, I try to move instead. The struggle doesn't lead anywhere, as I realize both my arms and legs are tied up.

All of a sudden, I hear footsteps. Their sound echoes around me as they come closer, but I can't figure out which direction they're coming from.

I focus harder, and through a fog, I hear something else in the distance, although barely audible. A sound of water running. I focus again, as hard as I can, but the only thing I can conclude is that it comes from the outside of this place.

*

I run as fast as my legs allow me to, tripping over tree branches and roots protruding from the ground. The night is too dark for me to see clearly enough where I'm headed, but I don't care. I need to escape.

I feel the chills, like someone is chasing me, but there's no one behind me. Who would even chase me?

They.

Who are they? I don't know the answer to that. The only thing I know is that I have to save someone. I don't know who that someone is either, but I need to get somewhere safe. Once I'm safe, I'll come back and save them. But come back where?

My knees buckle and I fall to the ground. Wet forest floor greets me as my legs give out.

No, this is wrong. I need to get up. I need to keep moving.

I see concrete not too far ahead. A road. I muster all the strength I have and swing my arm forward, grabbing at mud and wet grass. Inch by inch, I push myself closer to the road, but my arms are too weak. My breath becomes irregular as I tell myself I need to keep my eyes open. Just a little more...

But the world around me goes black.

*

When I get back to my senses, the only thing I see in front of me is the floor. I fell down on my knees at one point. When did that even happen?

The floor moves and shakes beneath me, and the only sound I hear is that of my breathing, and I'm surprised Jasmine isn't knocking on my door yet to ask me if I'm alright. It feels too loud while it echoes around me, as if the entire world can hear it.

As I finally give out and lay on the carpet, I notice my hand is still gripping something. An imaginary golden key. The last one I needed.

Because I know where my parents are keeping Chris.

CHAPTER 12

I'm sitting on my bed, replaying the newfound memories inside my head. My heart still races wildly as I try to make some sense of them.

They're from that night. Well, at least the first two. I even saw Chris in the old park. We were hanging out there when they kidnapped us.

I think about the memory fragment I got after that one. There were footsteps, but there was also the sound of water nearby. I remember there's an old cottage not too far from the river, and it's been abandoned for years. It could be a perfect place to leave two teenagers, considering how isolated it is. That must be the place.

I'm not sure if they're still keeping him there, but it's the only clue I have so far, so I have to get there somehow and investigate. However, I know how dangerous this is, which means I cannot do it alone. My best bet is to sneak out of the house and go to the police station to find someone who could help me.

But first, I need to go downstairs and see what Jasmine is doing. If I'm going to run away, I need to make sure to buy myself some time and keep her away from my bedroom for a while.

I spot her in the living room, watching TV on the couch.

"Elainne, is that you?" she asks when she hears my footsteps approaching.

"Yeah, I came down to grab some water," I reply with the first excuse that comes to my mind. "Where's dad? Is he not back yet?"

"No, he called in and said he'll be staying later, they got a delivery today so he has some extra work in the storage." She gives a quick glance to the clock on the wall. "Although, he should probably be back soon."

"Oh, okay. My head hurts a little, so I'm just gonna drink some water and then go to bed earlier. I'll probably be asleep when he comes back."

I see her expression changing from relaxed to worried in a second. "Are the headaches starting again?" She turns around to look at me with her arms crossed over her chest, so I try to put on my best tired expression.

"I don't think so, I'll probably be fine after I get some sleep." I reply.

"Alright then, make sure to get some rest. Good night!" she says as I walk out of the room. Since I have an excuse to own up to, I go to the kitchen and pour myself some water, then go upstairs when I gulp it down.

I waste no time in changing my previous clothesfor some more comfortable sweatpants and a hoodie to help me sneak around and run easier. Then I grab as many shirts and pants as I can, dumping them all on the bed. It's a bit difficult, but I shape them in a humanoid lump. It won't be able to deceive anyone for too long, but it might buy me some time if Jasmine comes to check on me later. I cover the lump with the blanket, hoping for the best.

When that trick is done, I open the window and look down. The height is huge, and I'd probably get hurt if I fell, but I know I've done this numerous times before. I take a deep breath, and then carefully swing one leg outside, then the other. I tightly grip the window ledge as I turn my body around, trying to find a footing in the facade. When I find it, I slowly start making my way down.

When I'm a few feet away from the ground, I assess it's safe enough for me to jump, so I do that, hoping that the sound wasn't loud enough to alert Jasmine. I tiptoe around the house and sneak through my own backyard, until I'm on the street. As soon as I get out of the reach of the house, I run.

As I make my way towards the police station, I remember the dream from a few days ago. Please don't let them appear there somehow, please, please...

Fortunately, there's no sign of them when I run in, only people in uniforms roaming around the hallway.

I drag my feet to the reception desk. "I need to talk to someone," I say, but my voice is barely audible, hoarse from all the running.

"Elainne?" a voice asks behind me. I turn around, only to see the man I came here for.

"You!" I breathe out. "I recognize you. You were in the hospital." I'm aware that's not a proper way to speak to a policeman, especially one that's so much older than me, but my mind is incapable of saying anything else.

Luckily for me, he sees how exhausted I am, and only nods politely. "Officer Marsh. What brings you here, Elainne?"

"I know where Chris is," I blurt out, not even waiting for him to take me somewhere more private. "Or, well, at least where we used to be. You need to come with me."

"Are you sure? Where is it?" I notice a few pairs of eyes staring at us intently, noticing the change in inspector's attitude.

"Near the river. There's that old cottage. You probably know about it. That's the place."

"Do your parents know about this?" he asks, and I let out a bitter laugh.

"Of course they do!" I'm not sure what's so funny, but I laugh again, driven by a sudden wave of exhaustion. "They're the ones who put us there."

The confusion on his face is almost too visible, but before he says anything, I tell him what really happened when we were kidnapped.

"Look, Elainne," he begins after hearing my story, putting his hand on my shoulder in a fatherly gesture. "This is a very complicated case, and we've kept in touch with your doctors. They said that delusions are a possibility with your condition. We've all seen how worried your parents were while you were gone. I doubt that what you're saying is the truth."

His words are like a punch to the gut. "B-b-but i-it's true!" I stutter. "You have to come with me!"

But he ignores my pleads. "Are any of your parents home?"

"No," I reply coldly, "there's no one there."

"Oh, is that so?" he asks with a tint of mockery in his voice, and I realize that he's not buying into my lie. "Well, I'm gonna go and call your home number just in case to see if anyone's gonna pick up. Wait for me here." He takes a step back, and just as he's about to turn around and leave me here, I grab his sleeve.

"I know what happened to me! I remember it," I cry out in an attempt to convince him, but he only gently pushes my hand away.

"Elainne, look, I'm not saying you're doing this on purpose, but your mind can't discern the truth right now. Just calm down and wait for me here, I'll be right back," he says as he walks away, not sparing me a second glance. Damn it.

He's going to call her. She'll realize I escaped, and she'll come here to get me. And everything will be over.

No. I can't let that happen. I didn't come all this way for nothing. I just need a plan to run away again before she arrives.

Two policemen stand at the door, their gazes locked on me from the distance, so I suppose that going back through the main entrance is not an option. I head further in until I'm out of their sight, and sit down on one of the waiting chairs in another hallway.

"Excuse me," I stop one of the policemen passing by while clutching my stomach. He looks only a few years older than me, and the name tag on his uniform tells me his name is Officer Jones. "Could you show me the way to the bathroom?"

"Sure thing, Miss, follow me," he agrees immediately, and I silently thank my luck for his gullibility as I get up and follow his lead. "You're Elainne, right? The girl who was kidnapped?"

"Yeah," I confirm reluctantly. I can only hope that he wasn't anywhere nearby while I was talking to Officer Marsh a few minutes ago.

"Oh, nice. I mean, not nice, obviously, but, you know," he says awkwardly, as if I'm supposed to know what that means.

"My grandpa is actually the one who found you in the woods and took you to the hospital." There's a moment of silence between us as I take my time to process what he says. "I'm sorry if that sounds a bit out of the blue," he apologizes instantly. "He likes hunting, so he frequents the area often, that's how he found you."

Hearing his words, I realize that I truly never knew anything about the person who found me and saved my life. All I was told was that it was a man, and that's about it. By the time I woke up in the hospital, the police already interrogated him, and he was free to go afterwards. "No, no, don't worry about it. Please thank him for me. I owe him a lot."

"I will." He nods solemnly. "So, what brings you here?" he asks.

I let out a fake sigh and try to play innocent. "Oh, I thought I remembered some useful information for the investigation and I wanted to tell Officer Marsh about it, but he doesn't think it's that valuable, so now I'm just waiting for my parents to come here and take me back home."

The young officer frowns upon hearing my words. "It's a bummer that your intel was a dead end. But don't worry, it may not look like it, but we're still working on the case, so hopefully we'll have some progress soon." Before I have the chance to thank him for the reassurement, he stops in front of a door with a toilet sign on it. "Alright, we're here. This is a staff bathroom, so if anyone asks you why you're there, tell them Officer Jones brought you here. You're not a convict, so it's not a big deal, and let me tell you, this bathroom is a lot cleaner than the other one we have."

I giggle at his words, even though they're exactly what I was hoping to hear. "Got it. Thanks a lot. Don't forget to say thanks to your grandpa for me!"

"Will do. See you around!" He waves as he leaves me behind and continues his route, so I waste no time in slipping through the door. .

When I get inside, the bathroom seems empty. I peek over the stall dividers until I spot what I need. I knock on the stall door, but there's no answer, so I push the door open and lock myself inside. Then turn around, looking at the window above me.

It's not that large, but I think I could squeeze through it with some effort. What's even better is that I don't see any bars on the outside.

I climb onto the lavatory lid that slightly bends under the pressure, and twist the handle, letting the chilly night air greet me. I look at the concrete not too far below me, bracing myself for another window escape. Seriously, if I have to crawl out of another window tonight, I won't even bother landing on my feet.

I push myself up, leaving the hardest part of work to my arms. First my head peaks out of the window, and I breathe a little sigh of relief when I see no one around. I push my feet against the wall for support as I try to squeeze my torso—the hardest part of my window escapade—through the window.

It takes a lot of wriggling, but inch by inch, I only have to swing my legs over the windowsill and jump down. I underestimate how hard it is to do that final step in such a narrow place, but I succeed after some struggle, and finally plummet down to the ground. I thank all the weight I've lost after the kidnapping as I roll over the concrete. Luckily for me, there's no one outside. When I get back to my feet, I take a few seconds to figure out the right direction, and then I flee.

If they don't want to follow me willingly, I'll make them follow me.

The cottage is even further from the police station than my house is, and I was already exhausted enough, so I start losing my breath after just a little bit of running. By the time I get to the river, I'm completely breathless, so I take a few minutes to calm down and regain my breath.

I jog forward, and the cottage soon comes into my field of vision. Slowly approach it, inspecting the area at the same time.

There's no sign of other people; no cars, no noise, no visible footprints. I approach the cottage carefully, and open the old, rusty door. It creaks as it moves in its hinges, the sound of it sending the shivers through my entire body.

I step inside, but don't get too far when I feel something. A touch of cold metal against the back of my head.

"Hello, Elainne."

CHAPTER 13

"I 've been expecting you,"Theodore says from behind me. I should've expected him as well, since he already lied about working overtime once, but I hoped this time it would be real. "Your mother called me and told me what you did, you little rat."

He instructs me to go forward, up the friable staircase. With every new step, my heart starts racing faster. My chances of overpowering him alone are very slim at best, but doing so when he has a gun is nearly impossible.

When we reach the top of the stairs, I see two rooms on the opposite sides. He leads me into the right one, and as soon as we enter, I see a body crumpled on the hard wooden floor.

"Chris!" I yell out and try to run to his side, but Theodore grabs my hand and yanks me back. He turns me around so that my back is pressed onto the opposite wall, and I yelp at the impact. He stands a few steps away from me, not a lot, but just enough to block my way with ease.

"Why are you doing this?" I scowl at him. If I want to get Chris out of here, I need to stall until my brain starts working fast enough to come up with a plan. Hopefully, the police found out I ran away by now and will try to follow me here.

Theodore scowls back at me, but his eyes are full of amusement, unlike mine. "What do you think?"

"Because you're narcissistic psychopaths," I spit out, and then yelp again when he slaps me across the cheek.

"Let me ask you one question in return. Did you pretend to have no memories this whole time, or did you just remember everything?"

I sneer at him while cupping my cheek. "Don't be stupid, if I knew everything from the start, I would've come here sooner.""Don't talk to me like that!" He slaps me again, and this time my knees buckle. I'm grateful that I have a wall behind me as support. "When did you remember?"

"Why would I tell you?"

"Because," he says, leisurely turning the gun in Chris's direction, "one bullet is enough to kill him on the spot. It would be a real shame for that to happen after you worked so hard to get here."

The panic must be clear on my face, because he laughs as I blurt out, "Two days before the doctor's appointment." I look at Chris's unconscious body on the floor, trying not to pay attention to Theodore's triumphant expression. "Why were you keeping him here this whole time?"

"Well, we couldn't just let him go after you tattled every-thing to him, right? But don't worry, your little boyfriend isn't seriously hurt... just a little starved."

Just when I'm about to reply, we hear the sound of footsteps echoing downstairs. He grabs my hand and drags me to the other side of the room, gesturing to stay quiet. We shield Chris's unconscious body as he puts a gun to my temple.

The footsteps approach slowly but confidently, as if the person knows exactly where they're headed. Both of us hold our breaths in anticipation, when Jasmine walks into the room.

"Oh, it's you," Theodore sighs, letting me go.

She doesn't pay any attention to him, fixing her ven-omous gaze onto me. "You little brat!" she growls, turning to Theodore. "That stupid officer said they won't do anything until I come and pick her up, but if she escaped them, they might be on their way here soon." For the first time, I pray that she's right and that Officer Marsh is on his way here.

"It's all your fault. You were supposed to keep an eye on her!"

A bitter laugh leaves my mouth, interrupting their quarrel. "Is that all I am to you? Something to keep an eye on? Your little pet?"

Jasmine glares at me. "I gave birth to you! Your life is in my hands!"

"Our hands," Theodore adds.

"That's not the way to treat your own child!" I cry out. "I'm not your pet, I'm a person! I shouldn't be a little copy of you that you get to control my entire life because you think that's the best way to fulfill your selfish desires." With every new word, I feel a huge weight disappear from my chest. Adrenaline gives me the strength I always needed to tell them everything I want. I'd confront them occasionally, but I had to stop myself from going too far every time. No matter what happens at the end of the night, I don't need to do so anymore.

"I've been putting up with your garbage treatment my entire life, and I'm sick of it! The only time I've had some piece in my life was when I lost my memories and couldn't remember how sick in the head you are." My voice cracks just when a tear slips out of my eye and rolls down my cheek, but I don't let that stop me. "Who would even go as far as to kidnap their own child just because they wanted a better life for themself? And when you found out I lost my memories and couldn't remember anything, the first thing you did was try to brainwash me again? And not only that, but you've also taken hostage of the only person who's ever treated me with respect and actually wanted to help me. I hate you," I hiss. "I freaking hate you!"

"Will you shut up already?" Jasmine retorts as if I haven't said anything. With shaky hands, I silently wipe the tears off of my face.

"No, both of you shut up!" Theodore shouts at us and then turns to Jasmine, completely ignoring me. "Did you hear that?"

"Hear what?"

We all stand still for a few moments before he says, "Nothing, I must've imagined something." He shakes his head, then points at Chris. "Get the boy and let's go."

She walks over to him and tries to pick him up. I expect her to struggle considering his weight, but he must've lost a lot of it in the meantime since she gets him on his feet with ease. I look at the domineering smile plastered on her face as she stares right at me.

Theodore doesn't say anything, and only grips my hands firmer, nodding towards the door. It looks like they notice the footsteps a second too late, because as soon as the two of them start dragging us towards the door, five policemen block the exit, pointing guns at my parents.

CHAPTER 14

"D on't get an inch closer, or I'll shoot her," Theodore barks as he puts the gun against my temple once again.

I look over to the policemen, and see Officer Marsh in the front, along with the younger officer who took me to the bathroom. There's a few more of them, and they're still holding their guns up, but not getting any closer to us as Theodore instructed.

"You know," Marsh says, "at first I didn't believe the girl when she told us what happened. I thought her head was still unclear, tried to listen to the doctors instead. But I didn't expect to be in the wrong about this." He stops, looking at him in disgust. "We all tried our best to find her for you, because of your desperate act. Were you really the ones behind all of this the entire time?"

"Oh, come on. You don't have any children, you can't under-stand this," Theodore retorts, as if holding your own child to a gunpoint is a completely normal thing to do.

"You're right, I don't. But I have a pregnant wife at home, and when my son is born, I can guarantee that I'll never treat him like this."

They stare at each other for what feels like an eternity, and nobody makes a move. I can only guess that Jasmine is in the same position too, since I can't see what's going on behind me, but I don't hear any sounds coming from her. There's only an awkward silence as we all wait for something to happen.

"Look," Officer Marsh decides to break the silence, "the back-up is on its way. If you want, we can stay like this for a little longer, but we're getting nowhere. You'll be surrounded soon, so lower your gun and knife and let the kids go." Knife? Theodore's gripping me with one hand and holding the gun in another, so with a tinge of panic I realize Jasmine is probably the one who has the knife. She could hurt Chris at any moment, and I probably wouldn't even see it.

"Then I guess we'll all go down together." Theodore stays determined as he presses the gun closer to my head. I wince at the impact, but he pays no attention to me. "It's a shame, you know. We never planned to kill her."

I look at Officer Marsh, who glares at Theodore cautiously. Even though he's at the front of the group, it seems that everyone is following his example. My gaze flies over the group, looking for anyone whose attention is on me. Finally, I spot that younger officer nervously glancing back and forth between Theodore and me.

Save Chris, I mouth to him. He seems to understand what I'm trying to say, and gives me a barely noticeable nod before he flashes a look behind me. For a split second, I think I see a confused expression written all over his face, but when I blink, his eyes are back on me and he looks just as nervous as he did before that.

I sense that Theodore is about to say something, but he's interrupted by a loud yelp coming from behind us, and a sound of metal hitting the wooden floor. I can't turn around to see what's going on behind me, but he does, and I feel his grip on me loosena bit as he tries to understand what's happening.

I grab my chance without thinking and gather all the strength I have left in my body to wrench out of his arms. I knock the gun out of his hand and hear a surprised grunt from him as Officer Marsh runs to his side and handcuffs him with lightning speed. Another two policemen tackle Jasmine, while Chris is crumpled on the floor again.

Breathing. Blinking. Moving.

The realization slowly breaks through my hazed mind. He's awake.

"Chris!" I dodge the other officers, who are walking behind Jasmine and Theodore, leading them outside. I kneel by his side, hugging him tightly.

"El... Elainne," he mumbles against my shoulder, and tears of relief finally break out of me. He tries to wrap his arm around me as I sob into his tattered shirt, but I don't need to be a medical expert to see how weak he is. We hug each other as the police sirens wail outside.

"Shhh, it's okay," I say as I rub his back. "We're safe. We're safe now."

Chapter 15

I look through the window of the cottage, watching the officers put my parents in the back of a police car, and then drive away. As if on cue, one siren is replaced with another when the ambulance arrives, and a few technicians soon join us in the room, only to put Chris on a stretcher and carefully carry him back downstairs. Officer Jones reluctantly follows them, leaving me alone with a disappointed Officer Marsh.

"I'm sorry for not trusting you from the start, Elainne," he says after a long silence. "I really thought they were the good guys. Since the day you disappeared, they were trying to get us to search for you two, even joined our search parties and kept in touch with us every day. We all believed they were good people. Now I see that was probably just a part of their plot to lead us astray."

I'm not sure what part of his words does it, but something breaks a dam inside of me, and the tears roll down my face again. I sniff into my sleeve while the officer awkwardly stands by my side.

My tears subdue a bit only after he gives me a short pat on the back. "Look, kiddo, you have to believe in what you said to your friend. You two are safe now. We'll all try our best to keep it that way."

The hospital hallway stretches far and wide ahead of us. I feel as if I'm pushed back through time, to the days when I was recovering in this same place. Officer Marsh is waiting with me in front of the hospital room where Chris is slowly coming back to his senses. The doctor is inside, and I can't help but fear that he'll suddenly walk out and relay some bad news to us.

I shiver as two sets of footsteps echo in the hallway, headed in our direction. I look up and see his parents running over to us, with a mixture of panic and relief written all over their faces.

"Elainne!" Jia Zhou rushes to my side, grabbing my shoulders. "Elainne! What happened? How is he? Will he be alright?" She fires out question after question, and I don't even have the time to answer before the door of Chris's room open and the doctor walks out.

"Are you the patient's family?" he asks the three of us, skipping the officer who's still in his recognizable police uniform. His parents nod urgently, and from the edge of my consciousness I find myself nodding too, even though I don't know why. "You can go inside to see him now, but I wouldn't advise spending too much time with him. It would be the best for him to rest." With those words, he promptly leaves us all in the hallway.

"Elainne," the officer's voice snaps me out of my thoughts, "do you want to head inside first? I'd like to tell his parents what happened first."

I look at the couple, and despite their impatient expressions, they silently agree. My hands tremble as I grab the door's handle, hesitating for a slight second before heading in.

The first thing I see is Chris, laying in his bed and staring at the ceiling. His eyes open and close slowly, revealing just how tired he is. I close the door behind me, and his head turns in my direction. He smiles, but I can't ignore the weary look of his face.

Tears well in my eyes as I run up to his bed, trying to hug him without moving his IV. We stay like that for a few minutes, my tears damping his hospital gown.

"I'm sorry," I finally murmur in his shoulder. "This is all my fault."

"Hey," he whispers, rubbing my back as I cry, "you saved my life."

"But I'm the one who put it in danger in the first place."

He pats my back lightly. "It's okay. It's not your fault."

"How are you feeling?" I ask him and put some distance between us, giving him some space as I wipe my tears.

"I'm better now that the drugs are wearing out," he replies, slumping deeper into his hospital bed.

"What even happened back there in the cottage?" I finally ask, since the time I spent with Officer Marsh was mostly full of awkward silence.

"Oh, I actually woke up in the meantime. You know, when police was already there and trying to stop your parents. It took a bit for my brain to start working again, but when I figured out your mother was the one holding me, I just swung my head back as hard as I could and hit her."

I stare at him dumbfounded. "That's actually impressive. Especially considering how weak you are."

"I mean, I'm pretty sure it hurt me more than it did her," he says with a tint of amusement in his voice. "But I hope I broke her nose or something." I chuckle at his ever the same joking tone, but it doesn't last for long.

"Did they-did they hurt you?"

"No, only kept me unconscious. Except when they gave me some food. To be honest, I was just sleeping most of the time." He giggles weakly, trying to lighten up the mood again, but I don't join him this time. "What happened to you?"

I take a deep breath, and then tell him the entire story, leaving nothing out for the first time.

After a minute of deadly silence, he finally speaks. "Elainn e... you're freaking brilliant, you know that?"

"I was just very lucky," I murmur. "If I had less luck and didn't rely on some wild guesses, I would probably still be stuck with them." I freeze at my own words, slowly realizing just how true that actually is. I had a lot of luck because every clue was still in its place. If at least one tiny element of the equation was changed in the meantime, I would've never found the flash drive and gotten my memories back.

"No, no, you're both lucky and brilliant, okay? I always told you you should become a detective," he teases.

I burst into laughter when I hear the door behind me open. I turn around, only to see his parents rushing in.

"Chris!" Jia yells and runs to his son's side. My heart clenches when I look at them, and I shift my gaze onto the worn out floor beneath me.

"I'm really sorry," I tell them, but I don't dare to look at their worried faces.

A hand reaches my shoulder and pats it gently. "This isn't your fault," Logan answers. "We noticed something wasn't quite right about your parents, but we weren't sure what to do. They seemed just as desperate as us."

I flinch when two arms suddenly wrap around me, enveloping me in a firm, but warm hug. "Thank you for saving his life," his mother sobs into my shoulder. Reluctantly, I return the hug. She's only a couple of inches shorter than me, but her hug makes me feel so much smaller in her arms.

After a minute, I awkwardly pull away and point towards the door. "I'll go outside and give you some privacy."

They don't argue, only nod and turn all their attention back to their son. I head towards the door, but stop when I grab the handle, turning around to look at them again. Chris isn't looking at me anymore, completely occupied by his parents who see nothing but him now.

With a painful pang in my chest, I realize that's what a family should be like—happy, united, supporting each other with nothing but love and good intentions in their hearts.

I think about those first days when I returned home, clouded by an illusion. I, too, had that, if only for a short while. But if everything was a lie, can I even call it a family?

With a corner of his eye, Chris glances at me, then locks his gaze with mine and gives me one of his flashy, but adorable smiles.

I smile back at him, then open the door and walk out.

Epilogue

What does the word family mean to me? Throughout my entire life, this was always one of the most difficult questions for me to answer. Involuntarily, my mind goes back to that day when I watched Chris reunite with his family in the hospital.

"Not ready to talk about that yet?" my therapist asks as I quietly wipe the tears off of my face.

"That's not the case," I claim, but my own words feel like a lie. "I just... I'm not sure."

We sit in silence for another minute, until I continue. "I guess I just feel ashamed and stupid for falling for their lies." I shrug and slump deeper into the chair, as if the motion will make me shrink and completely disappear.

"From your point of view, that's bad because you blame yourself for everything that happened. But I think you only 'fell for that' because you wanted to believe them; because, even when you had no memories of them, somewhere deep down you knew you deserved better than the treatment you were getting in the past."

I sit quietly, too stunned to say anything. The woman in front of me clearly takes that as a sign to continue. "You still need some time to process everything you went through and accept it. Even though it's been a few months since the incident resolved, there are years of unresolved past wounds underneath that. Things like those need a lot of time and patience, and you're the only one who can give that to yourself."

I fiddle with my fingers uncomfortably, pondering over her words. "But... what if I become like them someday?"

"We've already been over this, Elainne," she says firmly, but her voice still holds some gentleness to it. "By asking that question alone, you're showing effort to be different from them. And even if you have a trait or two in common, you are not your parents. You were under their shadow for too long, but you're still your own person, with thoughts and emotions of your own."

The minutes pass by as we both sit and wait for the other one to say something. After all, this is how most of our sessions worked—I usually spent more time sitting and thinking about her words than actually talking to her, but somehow, she said she can notice my progress.

"Should we change the topic to something brighter?" she asks after she's sure I have nothing else to add to the topic. "How are things going with Chris?"

"It's alright. He's fully recovered by now and got his weight back. But he's still stuck on that college thing."

"And why don't you want to go to college together?" Her careful eyes analyze me closely, hidden behind the rim of her glasses.

"I'm... not sure," I say in confusion. "I just don't think it's a good idea."

"Why not? Is it because he told you that he likes you?" she probes.

"Okay, that might be a reason," I admit weakly.

She smiles for a second, as if she expected that answer. "Do you think you're scared of getting attached to someone again?"

"No, no, that's not it," I deny immediately. "I mean, I'm already attached to him. He's been my best friend for years. Maybe that's the problem, because I see him as more of a family member. Especially now that I've lived with him and his family for the past couple of months."

After my parents' lies were uncovered and they were arrested, the Youngs were kind enough as to take me in and take care of me. I'm not sure if Chris somehow influenced that decision or not, but I'm grateful to them regardless. Despite me putting their son in danger, they've shown me nothing but kindness, which might be another reason why Chris having feelings for me just feels... weird.

"Regardless of that, we can have multiple families throughout our lives," my therapist continues. "First, we have our parents and blood relatives, but as we grow up, there are also people we're close with, then the loved ones we marry and start our own families with. Family isn't something that's fixed in stone and has only one meaning." I ponder over her words, but her voice interrupts me again. "Think about that until our next session."

I don't even realize how quickly time passed, because the session is already over, and I quickly get ready to leave her office. "Bye, Mrs. Adams!" I greet her and rush my shaky footsteps until I'm out on the street, soaking in the last lingering rays of fall sun. I take my phone out of my pocket and give a nervous glance to the screen. No new notifications.

I put it back into my pocket and continue forward, with the same old invisible gaze drilling holes into the back of my mind.